Dear Parent:

Congratulations! Your child is taking the first steps on an exciting journey. The destination? Independent reading!

STEP INTO READING® will help your child get there. The program offers five steps to reading success. Each step includes fun stories and colorful art. There are also Step into Reading Sticker Books, Step into Reading Math Readers, Step into Reading Phonics Readers, Step into Reading Write-In Readers, and Step into Reading Phonics Boxed Sets—a complete literacy program with something for every child.

Learning to Read, Step by Step!

Ready to Read Preschool–Kindergarten
• big type and easy words • rhyme and rhythm • picture clues
For children who know the alphabet and are eager to begin reading.

Reading with Help Preschool–Grade 1
• basic vocabulary • short sentences • simple stories
For children who recognize familiar words and sound out new words with help.

Reading on Your Own Grades 1–3
• engaging characters • easy-to-follow plots • popular topics
For children who are ready to read on their own.

Reading Paragraphs Grades 2–3
• challenging vocabulary • short paragraphs • exciting stories
For newly independent readers who read simple sentences with confidence.

Ready for Chapters Grades 2–4
• chapters • longer paragraphs • full-color art
For children who want to take the plunge into chapter books but still like colorful pictures.

STEP INTO READING® is designed to give every child a successful reading experience. The grade levels are only guides. Children can progress through the steps at their own speed, developing confidence in their reading, no matter what their grade.

Remember, a lifetime love of reading starts with a single step!

To Lucky, the original dinky dog
—K.K.

To Kendra, who always believed,
and Winston, who showed me
the way of the pup —M.F.

Text copyright © 2013 by Kate Klimo
Cover art and interior illustrations copyright © 2013 by Michael Fleming

All rights reserved.
Published in the United States by Random House Children's Books, a division of Random House, Inc., New York.

Step into Reading, Random House, and the Random House colophon are registered trademarks of Random House, Inc.

Visit us on the Web!
StepIntoReading.com
randomhouse.com/kids

Educators and librarians, for a variety of teaching tools, visit us at
RHTeachersLibrarians.com

Library of Congress Cataloging-in-Publication Data
Klimo, Kate.
Twinky the dinky dog / by Kate Klimo ; illustrated by Michael Fleming.
    p.   cm. — (Step into reading. Step 3)
Summary: "The world treats Twinky like a dinky dog. The only problem is that Twinky doesn't feel dinky. What can a little dog do to prove the age-old adage that size doesn't matter?"— Provided by publisher.
ISBN 978-0-307-97667-3 (trade pbk.) — ISBN 978-0-375-97122-8 (lib. bdg.) — ISBN 978-0-375-98115-9 (ebook)
[1. Dogs—Fiction. 2. Size—Fiction. 3. Self-perception—Fiction.] I. Fleming, Michael, ill. II. Title.
PZ7.K67896Tw 2013
[E]—dc23 2012016297

Printed in the United States of America
10 9 8 7 6 5 4 3 2 1

TWINKY
THE DINKY DOG

by Kate Klimo

illustrated by Michael Fleming

Random House New York

Twinky was a very big dog.

At least in his own eyes.

In the eyes of the rest of the world,

Twinky was dinky.

Twinky's owner treated him
like a dinky dog.

She carried him
like a purse.

She dressed Twinky up
in silly sweaters.

She sent Twinky
to charm school.

She called him
Twinky-Poo!

And she made him go potty
on a wee-wee pad.
That was the worst!

Twinky wanted to run

with the big dogs

in the big-dog park!

He dreamed of
curb and tree trunk
and new-mown lawn.
And long, wide sidewalks
in the misty dawn.

11

But Bubba and Tank
and Bertha wanted nothing
to do with Twinky.
Because his owner
carried him around
like a purse!

Because his owner
dressed him in silly sweaters!
Because his owner
called him Twinky-Poo!
Because his owner made him
go potty on a wee-wee pad!

Bubba and Tank

and Bertha

growled at dinky-dog things.

At dinky-dog treats
and dinky-dog tops.
Dinky-dog collars
and dinky-dog shops.

It was not fair.

In his heart Twinky knew

he was a big dog.

Was this any way to treat
a big dog?
No, it was not!
Twinky would show them!

He waited until his owner
was busy talking on the phone.
Then he wiggled
and jiggled loose.

18

He ran to the big-dog park
as fast as his dinky legs
could carry him.

The big dogs saw
dinky Twinky
out running loose.
They teased him!

Bubba asked where
his fancy collar was!

Tank asked where
his silly sweater was!

Bertha asked where
his wee-wee pad was!

Twinky told them

he had wiggled loose.

And now it was time for him

to learn the big-dog moves.

The big dogs
growled and scowled.
Then they put
their heads together.
Bubba looked at Tank.
Tank looked at Bertha.
Bertha looked at Bubba.

The big dogs agreed.

It was time

to teach Twinky

the big-dog moves.

They showed Twinky
big-dog struts

and big-dog growls.
Big-dog snarls

and big-dog scowls.

Twinky was getting
the hang of it.

But then his owner found him.
She had been looking all over
for her Twinky-Poo.

Twinky was sad that
he had to go home.

Twinky tried out
the big-dog moves
when he got home.

He tried the struts and growls

and snarls and scowls.

Sometimes he even scared himself!

Bit by bit,
Twinky began to feel
like a big dog.

Then there came
a dark and stormy night.

Twinky heard a scary noise
outside the door.
So did Twinky's owner.

It was a robber!

Twinky's owner was scared!

She reached for her phone

to call the police.

But she couldn't find it!

Growl rose to bark
and bark rose to ROAR!!!!!
Twinky sent that robber
running for his life.

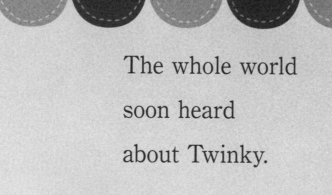

The whole world
soon heard
about Twinky.

His picture was
on the front page
of the newspaper.

Things changed for Twinky.
No more being carried
around like a purse.
No more silly sweaters.
No more charm school.
And no more wee-wee pad.
That was best of all.

Now Twinky ran
with the big dogs.
With Bubba and Tank
and Bertha.

Now Twinky enjoyed
curb and tree trunk

and new-mown lawn.

And long, wide sidewalks

in the misty dawn.

Twinky was NOT dinky.

And now

the whole world knew it.